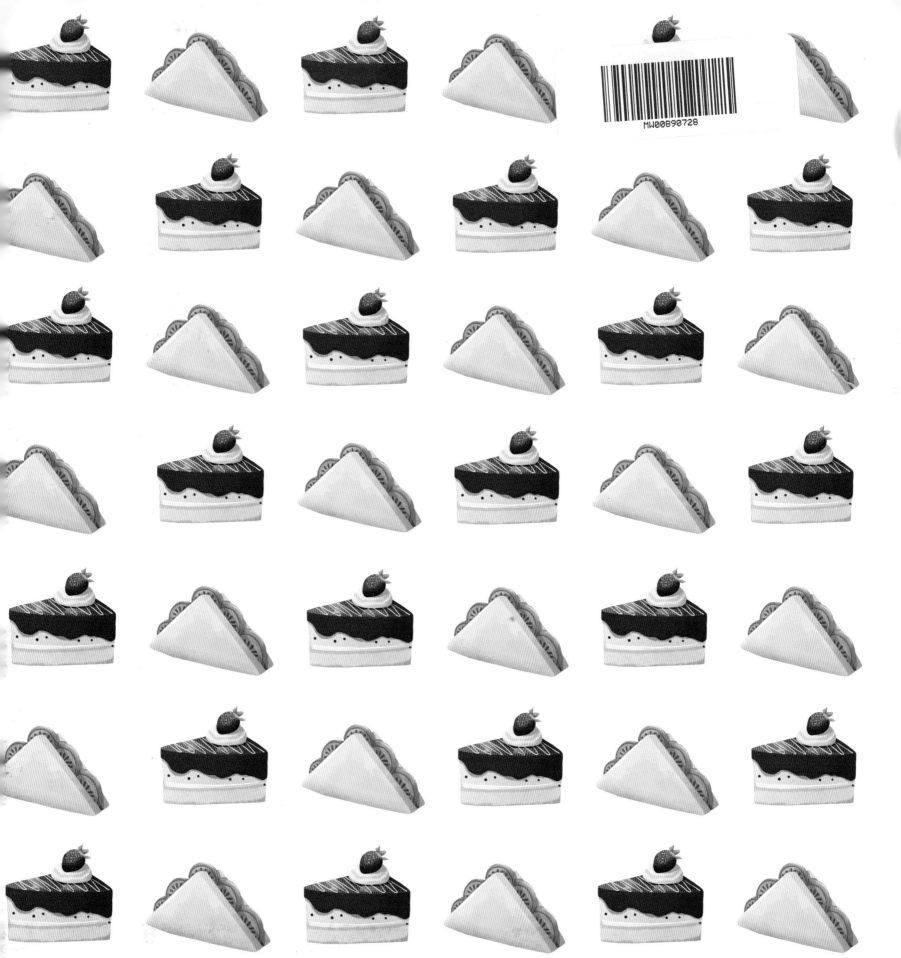

© 2021 Sunbird Books, an imprint of Phoenix International Publications, Inc.
8501 West Higgins Road   59 Gloucester Place
Chicago, Illinois 60631   London W1U 8JJ

www.sunbirdkidsbooks.com

Library of Congress Control Number: 2020945245

ISBN: 978-1-5037-5711-0 Printed in China

The art for this book was created digitally.
Text set in Century Old Style with flourishes of Active, DIN Condensed, CCSignLanguage, Goodlife Serif, Snell Roundhand, Chelsea Market Pro, Kirsten Normal ITC, and Chaloops.

UNICORNS
HAVE BAD MANNERS

Written by Rachel Halpern
Illustrated by Wendy Tan Shiau Wei

sunbird books

Nigel loves tea parties! But he is very fussy about etiquette, even for a dinosaur…and you know how dinosaurs can be. Nigel has searched and *searched* for someone with manners as perfect as his own. But he has always been disappointed.

He dined with a dragon who wouldn't say please, and set the whole table on **fire** when she **sneezed**.

AH-choo!

He once saw a llama **pour tea** on his bread, then **balance a teacup** on top of his head.

Last month he tried serving an octopus lunch, but they **juggled** their apples and **gargled** their punch.

But today will be different. Today, Nigel's guest is a

UNICORN.

Nigel knows a unicorn's manners will be sublime.

Just as Nigel places the last spoon on the table,
PERIWINKLE,
his soon-to-be-best-unicorn-friend, arrives!

Nigel puts his napkin on his lap with a *flourish*.
Periwinkle…**doesn't**.

"Would you care for something to sip?" Nigel asks. "Perhaps—"
"WOULD I!" Periwinkle says, and she grabs the soup ladle
before Nigel can say *a spot of tea*. But Periwinkle doesn't *sip* her soup...

"I thought you might…want some tea…" Nigel says weakly.
"Oh!" Periwinkle says. "Don't mind if I do."
She reaches across the table
to stab a stack of cookies…

"It's nice to meet new people, isn't it?" Periwinkle says, twirling her fork. "I'm so glad you invited me."

Nigel is **NOT** glad. Nigel has to take a deep breath and eat a soothing cucumber sandwich.

That's when
Periwinkle says,

"Ooh, lilacs!"

...and eats the flowers
right out of the vase.

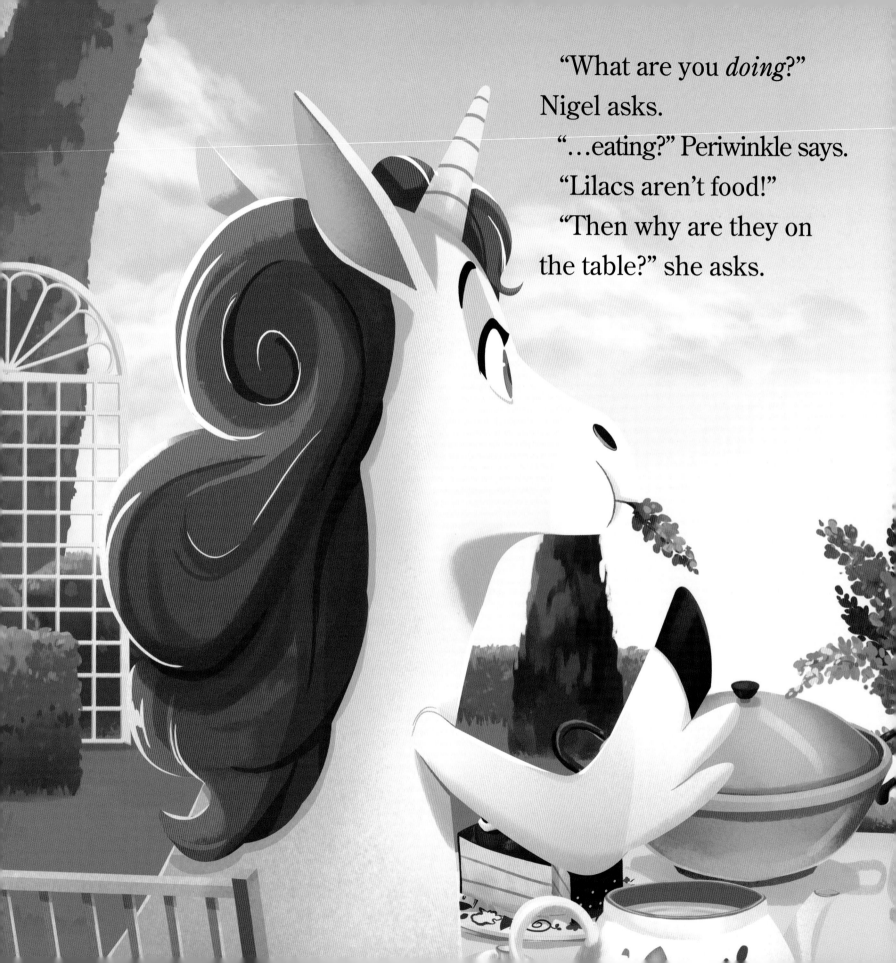

"What are you *doing*?" Nigel asks.

"...eating?" Periwinkle says. "Lilacs aren't food!"

"Then why are they on the table?" she asks.

"You ate the centerpiece! You drank the soup! You dipped cookies in the teapot! You didn't even put your napkin on your lap!" Nigel buries his face in his hands.

"I thought a unicorn would be **POLITE** and **REFINED**.
I thought we'd nibble cucumber sandwiches and—and sip
tea with our pinkies out!"

"But I **CAN'T** stick my pinky out!" Periwinkle says. "I have **HOOVES**! And **EVERYONE** dips their cookies in their tea."

"They very much **DO NOT!**" Nigel says.

"Then they **SHOULD**," Periwinkle says. "**IT'S DELICIOUS!**"

"Anyway, I think it's pretty rude to shout about your guest's manners," Periwinkle says, more calmly.

"I didn't say anything when you
ate a sandwich before dessert."

"Wait," Nigel says, "you're *supposed* to eat dessert last."

"My great-grandma Gardenia wouldn't approve of that," Periwinkle says primly. "Imagine! It would be like— eating cookies without a fork! Or putting soup in a bowl!"

"Why wouldn't you put soup in a bowl?" Nigel asks.

"Because," Periwinkle says, "it's just **bad manners!**"

"But...don't you think it's rude to eat straight from the pot?"

"I did wonder why it only had one ladle," Periwinkle says thoughtfully.

"What about reaching across the whole table?" Nigel asks.

"But if you don't," Periwinkle says, "someone has to hand you everything!"

"Slurping your soup?"

"Cools it down faster!"

"Putting your elbows on the table?"

"Now I *know* you're just making these up," Periwinkle says.

"Why wouldn't you put your elbows on the table?"

Nigel tries putting his elbows on the table.
It really *is* a bit of a silly rule.
"I never use a fork when *I* eat cookies,"
he says.

"Well, in that case…" Periwinkle says, and she takes a cookie with one dainty hoof.

Nigel nibbles on
a lilac blossom.

Periwinkle tries eating
her soup with a spoon.

MUNCH
MUNCH

The cookies really *are* delicious when Nigel dips them in his tea.

sssssLLLLLURRRP

…but Nigel still saves dessert for last.